Contents

1 The Strange Creature............................1

2 The Creature – Again! 5

3 Looking for Answers 11

4 The Search...22

5 Back on the Trail 32

6 Big Foot, At Last................................37

CHAPTER 1

Gold Fever

The creature looked like a huge black bear or a dark monster. It moved away from the two young men and disappeared in the trees.

Carlos Mendez and P.J. Turner did not move. They stared at one another.

The creature made a loud strange sound as it turned and ran away from them.

"Wow!" said Carlos softly.

"What was that?" P.J. asked.

"I don't know. I've never seen anything so big," Carlos said.

"How big did it look to you?" P.J. asked.

"I don't know. In the dark it looked 15 feet tall," Carlos replied.

"Well, I know one thing, Carlos. I am

leaving here now! Next time we decide to go fishing, I'm going to pick another spot," P.J. said. He began to put his clothes and fishing gear into his bag.

Carlos thought for a moment. "You know, P.J., maybe this could get our names in the paper."

"What are you talking about?" P.J. asked.

"I mean maybe that big strange creature is well known. Maybe it has scared other people just the way it scared us," Carlos said.

P.J. said, "And maybe you're crazy."

Carlos put another stick of wood on the fire. "I think we should try to find out more about the creature," he said.

P.J. closed his bag. "Pack your bag, Carlos. Let's get out of here right now."

"P.J., that animal won't come back here tonight. Let's stay the night," Carlos said.

"Why?" P.J. wanted to know.

Carlos unrolled his sleeping bag. "Because

we came here for the weekend. I want to stay at least two nights, and maybe we'll see the creature again."

"I don't want to see it again," P.J. said crossly.

"Come on, P.J. Just one more night," Carlos begged.

P.J. stopped what he was doing for a moment. He seemed to be thinking it over. Then he said, "Well, I don't want to but I will," He began to unpack his bag. "I'm only staying because it will give us a chance to fish again tomorrow. I hope we catch more than we did today."

"We'll fish early in the morning. That's when they bite best," Carlos said as he rolled over in his sleeping bag.

P.J. got into his sleeping bag, too. He wanted to go home but he knew that Carlos would never rest until he found out more about the strange creature.

Carlos fell asleep very fast. But P.J. stayed awake listening to the sounds of the night. What would happen tomorrow, he wondered. Would they see the strange creature again? Did they really even see it in the first place?

P.J. finally fell asleep with the campfire burning brightly nearby.

CHAPTER 2

The Creature – Again!

Early the next afternoon P.J. said, "We've caught our limit of fish for the day. Why don't we spend some time looking around? Then next time we come, we'll know more about the woods."

"Sounds great to me. And if we take a walk, we may get another look at that strange creature," Carlos said.

They walked a long distance along the top of a hill. Finally, P.J. said, "Let's stop for a little while."

"Good idea," Carlos agreed.

They sat down on some smooth rocks. From this point they could see across a small valley where Little River ran. The green trees and grasses of spring were all around. They rested and enjoyed the view for more than an hour.

Late in the afternoon they returned to their camp. They went to the river's edge, took the fish basket out, and selected a few fish to clean and cook for their evening meal. They baked some potatoes in the coals of the fire. They toasted marshmallows for dessert.

Night came and the hours moved by slowly. They talked and waited for time to pass. Would the strange creature come back? It had been midnight when they saw it the night before.

At last Carlos said, "P.J., it's time to go."

They walked with their small flashlights shining in the dark. A little way from camp Carlos whispered softly, "This is where we saw the creature last night."

P.J. whispered back, "Yes. I wonder if it will be here again tonight."

They sat down behind a rock near where

they had seen the creature the night before. The rock was almost 8 feet high and behind it were thick woods. They sat for what seemed like a long time.

After midnight Carlos said, "I don't think it is coming here tonight."

P.J. said quickly, "Hush, Carlos. I think I hear something."

A soft sound seemed to be coming from the woods. It slowly grew louder. The sound was like a person or an animal walking slowly, crushing leaves and twigs as it moved.

As the creature got nearer it seemed to be making soft grunting and breathing sounds.

P.J. and Carlos heard something scratching against their rock. Slowly it climbed onto the rock from the back side, away from where they sat. Then they saw a long arm and claw waving above the rock against the sky. The animal was standing on top of the rock!

Suddenly, as planned, P.J. and Carlos

jumped up from their hiding place and shined their flashlights on the creature.

They were not sure what they saw. It looked like a large animal 10 feet tall. It seemed to have a very small head for such a huge creature.

The animal was so surprised by their lights that it stared a moment into the glare. Then it jumped off the rock and fled back into the woods. P.J. and Carlos tried to chase it. But they were on a loose gravel path and slipped when they tried to run. Soon they were left far behind.

"I didn't really want to get close to it," Carlos said.

"At least not close enough to shake hands. An animal that big could tear us apart," P.J. said.

They talked about the creature as they walked back to their camp.

"It really looked 10 feet tall," Carlos said.

"You're right. It sure did," P.J. said. "But

we must remember that it was on top of that rock. The rock is about 8 feet. We were much lower on the ground. So it could be easy for us to make a wrong guess about its size."

Carlos agreed. He said, "We didn't really get a good look at the animal when we were on the same level with it."

"Oh, well, we probably will never get so close again," P.J. said sadly.

They unrolled their sleeping bags and got ready for bed.

The next morning as they drove home, they were still talking about the creature. The more they talked, the more puzzled they became.

"Was it really an animal?" Carlos wondered.

"I don't know what else it could be," P.J. answered.

"But an animal that big? Why hasn't it been seen before? Are we the first ones ever to have seen it?" Carlos wondered.

"You're asking a lot of questions, Carlos," P.J. said.

"You're right! But they all need answers," Carlos said.

"Maybe we'll be the ones to get them," P.J. smiled.

CHAPTER 3

Looking for Answers

On Monday after the weekend fishing trip Carlos and P.J. talked during their lunch hour at the Watson Furniture Company.

As he sat down on one of the benches, Carlos said, "P.J., I've been thinking about that creature or whatever it was."

"Guess what, Carlos. I've been doing the same thing," P.J. said.

"I've decided that what we saw was Big Foot. Do you know about Big Foot?" Carlos asked.

P.J. thought for a moment. "I don't know much about Big Foot. Only that he is a huge unknown animal of some kind."

"That's all you need to know. People have

been seeing Big Foot tracks all over the West," Carlos said.

P.J. replied, "Now what do we do?"

Carlos said quickly, "Let's call the animal we saw Big Foot. It seems strange to go around saying 'the creature.' "

P.J. grinned. "O.K. We call it Big Foot. Then what?"

"Well, what do we know about our Big Foot?" Carlos asked. He did not wait for a reply but went on. "We know that it is big, maybe 10 feet tall. It looks something like a bear and lives in the forest."

"That sounds right to me, Carlos," P.J. said.

"Big Foot will be afraid to go back to that same rock again. I'd be afraid if someone jumped up and shined a light at me," Carlos added.

P.J. was thinking hard. "Carlos, do you think maybe what we saw isn't the real Big Foot?"

Carlos answered, "No. I didn't think of that. Why do you ask?"

P.J. said, "Oh, I don't know. The thing seemed somehow different to me. The way it ran didn't seem like any animal I've ever seen."

Carlos did not reply for a few moments. Then he asked, "What do you think we should do?"

P.J. said, "Next time we go out there we could stop at a store. Maybe the owner would know if Big Foot has been seen around there. Maybe we'd learn the names of some people who really know the woods."

"Hey, that sounds great. I'm in favor!" Carlos said.

Soon the whistle sounded for them to return to work. As they walked in, P.J. said, "We'll make plans for our next trip later in the week."

On the next Saturday they drove out in

Carlos's old car. They stopped at a small country store near Little River and went inside.

The owner of the store was Bill Crum. He said, "I've lived near here all my life. I've hunted in the woods hundreds of times."

*"I've lived near here all my life.
I never saw a bear that tall."*

"Did you ever see a very big bear?" Carlos asked.

"How big?" Mr. Crum asked.

"Maybe 10 feet tall," Carlos said.

"Nope. I never saw a bear that tall. That's taller than any animal I've seen in these woods," Mr. Crum replied.

P.J. asked, "Well, have you ever seen an animal that might be Big Foot?"

Mr. Crum smiled. "That idea again. No, I've never seen an animal like that. But two or three years ago Hal Spear said he saw one."

"Where does this man, Hal Spear, live?" P.J. wanted to know.

Mr. Crum told them how to find Hal Spear's cabin.

They turned off the main road onto a narrow, unpaved one. The road was very rocky and rough.

"Wow! I hope Mr. Spear knows a lot about Big Foot. That would repay us for bouncing over this road," Carlos said as he moved the steering wheel back and forth.

After a mile on the rocky road they found an old cabin. It was a few yards past the end of the road.

Carlos stopped the car and turned off the motor. They got out and walked toward the cabin.

Suddenly they heard a shot. Just in front of them dirt flew up from the ground where a bullet had hit.

A loud voice shouted, "Stop where you are!"

Carlos and P.J. stood without moving.

The voice said, "Put your hands up! I'm coming toward you."

They put their hands up.

The front door of the cabin opened. A man came out. He wore a faded shirt and overalls. As he came closer, they could see his red face.

"Who are you?" he asked when he got up close.

P.J. said, "I'm P.J. Turner. This is my friend, Carlos Mendez."

"What do you want?" the man asked.

*"Who are you?" he asked
when he came close to them.*

"We are here to see Hal Spear. Mr. Crum told us how to find you," P.J. said.

Now the man smiled. "All right. I'm Hal Spear. Bill Crum is a good friend. Put your hands down. Now what do you want from me?"

P.J. was nervous. "Mr. Crum told us that you saw Big Foot in the woods."

"Why don't you two come in the cabin? I've got soft drinks. We can talk for a while," Mr. Spear said. He dropped his gun to his side.

Carlos made a low sound, "Whew!"

Mr. Spear said, "I'm sorry if I scared you. Sometimes strange people come here. They like to laugh at me. They throw rocks at my cabin. But you two seem all right. Let's go inside and talk."

Carlos and P.J. followed him into the cabin. They sat down in chairs Mr. Spear pointed out to them.

The cabin was neat and clean. A low fire

burned in the fireplace. A kettle of soup was simmering on the black iron stove.

Mr. Spear laid his gun on a table. He took some cans of soft drinks out of an old wooden icebox.

Then he said, "So you've got Big Foot on your mind. Once over across the hills I missed seeing Big Foot by a few seconds. I heard it running away."

"Will you tell us anything you can remember, anything at all?" P.J. asked.

"I saw a big footprint in the sand. It was strange. The large foot hadn't sunk into the soft sand very much," Mr. Spear said.

"Why was that strange?" Carlos asked.

"A big, heavy animal should sink a bit into the sand," Mr. Spear said.

P.J. and Carlos sat and waited. They hoped Mr. Spear could tell them more.

He finally stood up and said, "Two years back a hunter told me that he had seen a strange animal. But that's all I know."

Carlos and P.J. finished their soft drinks and stood up to leave.

Carlos said, "Thank you very much." P.J. did the same.

They all talked as they walked toward Carlos's car.

Mr. Spear said, "I'm glad somebody is looking for Big Foot. You two are off to a great start."

Carlos said, "Well, we know we saw something twice last time we were in the woods. But it didn't look the same each time."

P.J. said quickly, "We saw it from two different angles. It could have been the same creature. We're just not sure. It all just doesn't add up quite right."

Mr. Spear nodded his head. "I've seen footprints more than once. They were not always the same size. Could there be a whole family of the creatures?"

"We don't know. We'll think about that," P.J. said.

"Thanks again, Mr. Spear," Carlos said. He drove back slowly over the narrow road to the park rangers' office.

They talked with Ranger Marsh, who had worked in the park woodlands for many years. He told them, "There are rumors of a Big Foot in these woods, but I've never seen it. You can look around. Just don't shoot anything. He gave them permits to camp and maps of the trails.

As they drove home, they were pleased with what they had learned, and they were full of plans.

CHAPTER 4

The Search

The next Saturday they drove back to the rangers' office at Green Mountain State Park and signed in as visitors for the day. They seemed to be the only campers that day.

"Let's leave your car here and walk along some of the trails. We may find something interesting," P.J. said.

They looked at the maps Ranger Marsh had given them. They decided to walk along a trail that went to the top of Green Mountain.

They saw some camping spots where people could pitch tents. A spring with pure water was near each camp. A rock stove with firewood was there for cooking. The camp spots did not look as if they were used very much.

Carlos said, "I wish I had a candy bar. I could eat a big one right now."

"I'm hungry, too. Let's sit here and eat our lunches," P.J. said.

Carlos asked, "By any chance did you bring an extra candy bar?"

"Sorry, no candy bar but I have an extra apple if you want it," P.J. said.

Carlos said, "Guess I'll eat one of my sandwiches first."

They ate slowly. They talked about the many places where Big Foot could hide. And there seemed to be a lot of them.

"Let's come back to this camp site next weekend. This could be a place that Big Foot likes," Carlos said.

"Good idea," P.J. agreed.

They stood up and dropped their waste paper into a trash can. Then they walked farther along the trail.

The next weekend they came back to the

same spot late on Friday afternoon. It was too dark to see clearly when they reached the camp. It was also rather cool. They lit a fire in the rock stove. They wore heavy coats to stay warm. They did not have a tent, only their sleeping bags.

Together they had filled a cooler with sandwiches, extra bread, and cheese.

"I hope we have plenty of food," Carlos said.

"I think we brought enough for Big Foot," P.J. said with a grin.

They rested at the camp for a couple of hours. Then with their flashlights they walked a short distance in each direction from the camp. They hoped to find a good place to stop and wait for Big Foot. They finally stopped near a large rock. It was like the large rock where they had seen Big Foot before.

They waited in this spot until after midnight. Big Foot did not come. They went back to their camp.

"Before they went to sleep, P.J. said, "Tomorrow we'll find a better place to watch from."

"Yeah," Carlos said in a sleepy voice.

The next morning they made their plans for the day. After breakfast they would walk farther along the trail and look for places Big Foot might like to go at night. They would also look for places where Big Foot might live.

As they walked, they marked places on their maps. Later in the morning they walked off the trail into the woods.

Carlos pointed to the left and said, "Look, P.J., that big rock over there seems like a good place for Big Foot."

"You're right, Carlos. Let's walk closer," P.J. said.

P.J. climbed up one side of the rock. Carlos climbed up another side.

"Hey, Carlos. There are scratches in the

rock. They could be places where Big Foot marked it with his claws," P.J. said. "Of course, a bear might have made them, too."

Carlos began looking carefully along the side of the rock. Soon he said, "Yes. The rock is marked here, too. I think this is the place we should watch tonight. What do you think, P.J.?"

P.J. said, "I agree. This is the best place we've seen today."

They climbed down from the rock and searched around its base. Now and then they found small tracks of rabbits and squirrels. But they found no big tracks in the rocky soil.

P.J. said, "We should leave this spot right now. If we stay very long, any animal that comes later might smell us and take off."

Carlos said, "We need to find a place to watch from, not too close and not too far away."

"I want to be close enough to take a good picture when you shine your light on Big Foot,"

P.J. said.

"I hope that camera you rented is a good one," said Carlos.

P.J. took the camera out of his back pack. He said, "I think it is a good one. I'll take some shots of the rock to try it out. This camera has a flash bulb."

"So?" Carlos asked.

"So it will help us get a clear photo. The camera salesman showed me how to do it," P.J. said. "I'm pretty sure I remember what he said. Let's move back a little way."

After looking around they found a small clearing from which they could watch the rock.

"This looks like a perfect place to watch from," Carlos said.

They ate their sandwiches early. They wanted no scent of food around if Big Foot came their way. They settled down to wait.

They whispered softly as they waited. There was some light from the moon. They could see a short distance.

Some time after midnight they decided Big Foot was not coming. They spread out their sleeping bags and quit watching.

Just at daybreak a sharp sound awakened P.J. He sat up. A large dog was barking near him. It growled between barks.

P.J. was surprised. He began to slide out of his sleeping bag. The dog was only a few feet away. P.J. tried speaking in soft, friendly tones to calm the animal. He stood up with his sleeping bag in his hand. The dog jumped toward him. P.J. tossed his sleeping bag into the dog's face.

Just then Carlos stood up. The dog was scared by the sudden move. It ran a short distance. Then it stopped and barked again.

They heard a loud voice from down the trail calling, "Blackie, come here, boy!"

The dog stopped barking. It sat down and waited nearby.

P.J. and Carlos heard someone walking along the trail. Soon a person wearing woodsman's clothes walked up. After a moment the person took off the heavy cap. P.J. and Carlos were surprised. It was a woman.

A large dog was barking near him.
The dog looked angry.

She spoke first to the dog. "Blackie, stop bothering people. They were here first."

Then she turned to P.J. and Carlos and said, "I'm sorry. I hope he didn't hurt anyone."

P.J. said, "No real harm. He scared me. I'm glad you came when you did. We didn't expect to see anyone in the park this early."

"Well, you could see me here any time," she said.

P.J. told her their names.

The woman said, "My name is Mary Sue. I live just over that way." She pointed down the trail. Carlos and P.J. had not walked that way yet.

P.J. said, "We've got some bread and cheese. Would you like some?"

Mary Sue shook her head and said softly, "No thanks."

Before P.J. or Carlos could decide what to say next, she began to walk away. She called to her dog, "Come, Blackie, let's go home."

She and the dog walked back down the trail.

"Wow! She's a bit strange," Carlos said.

P.J. frowned and said, "Yes, but we probably seemed strange to her, too."

CHAPTER 5

Back on the Trail

On Monday P.J. and Carlos were back at work. During their lunch break they talked more about the weekend.

P.J. said, "I'm not surprised we didn't find Big Foot. Some people have spent years looking for strange creatures. But I was surprised to see that dog and woman in the park."

"I think she may know something," Carlos said.

"Let's go back on Saturday and try to find her again," P.J. said.

"That may not be easy. Remember, the rangers didn't know her," Carlos said.

"Maybe she lives on the far side of the park from the rangers' office," Carlos said.

"O.K. We'll check her out if we can," P.J. replied.

On Saturday morning Carlos and P.J. drove along the state highway past Little River to the far side of the park. After a few miles they asked directions at a gas station.

A man there told them to drive two more miles, then turn left. At the end of that road they would see a few houses.

They did exactly that. Carlos stopped his car at the end of the road. A trail led to some houses. No one answered when they knocked on the doors of the houses.

The sky was cloudy. A soft rain began.

P.J. looked at the sky and said, "Let's run over to those trees. We won't get so wet under the limbs. It's safe as long as there's no lightning."

Carlos said, "Look, maybe we can keep dry under those rocks over there."

They ran through the rain and found a dry

area against a slanted rock. In about half an hour the rain stopped.

They stood up, and P.J. walked around the rock. He called to Carlos from the back side, "Hey, Carlos, come here."

Carlos walked around the rock. On the back side there was a large hole that went right into the side of the rock.

"Hey! That looks like a cave," Carlos said.

"It is a cave. I looked in. There's stuff inside," P.J. said.

"Let's go in," Carlos said.

They walked into the cave. Their flashlights showed large boxes inside.

"Do you think somebody camps here?" Carlos asked.

P.J. replied, "I don't know. Let's look around a little more."

P.J. walked over to a box. He reached in and took out some animal skins. They looked like bear skins.

Carlos took the top from another box. He took out pieces of clothing. The two of them stared at each other. They were not quite sure what they had found.

"This is strange. Let's get out of here," P.J.

P.J. reached inside and took out some animal skins.

said. "The sooner, the better!"

They went back to the trail. At its end they found another house. A small sign on a post in the front yard had the name "Mary Sue" written on it.

"So this is where she lives," Carlos said.

P.J. pointed to the side of the house. A strong, low fence was there a few yards from the house. "That's the woods on the other side of the fence," he said.

"Wow! She lives very close to the woods," Carlos said.

"I think she is close to something else, too," P.J. said.

CHAPTER 6

Big Foot at Last!

They walked back to the car.

Carlos asked, "P.J., do you think Big Foot lives in that cave?"

"No. I don't think any animal or human lives there. I think the skins and clothes are there for a reason. I don't think Big Foot uses them. But I'm not sure who does," P.J. replied. "Or if it's an animal or a person."

Carlos looked surprised. "How could Big Foot be a person? Don't you remember that huge animal we saw?"

P.J. replied, "Well, it looked like an animal. But a person wearing bear skins, a mask, black tape, and other things could look like an animal."

Carlos said, "But we don't know that."

"You're right, we don't. But we might find out if we watched the cave. We might see an animal or a person go in and come out. Then we might learn what our Big Foot really is," P.J. said.

Carlos did not reply right away. He was thinking. Then he said, "We can't do it today. We didn't bring our sleeping bags or food. We might have to wait a long time."

"You're right," P.J. said. "We'll come back tomorrow. We'll hide somewhere and watch the cave."

Carlos said, "That's the only way we're going to find out for sure."

The next day they came back to the clump of trees near the big rock. Each of them carried a back pack and a sleeping bag. They unloaded among the trees because they didn't want to be seen. Carlos used his field glasses to watch the rock. He would be able to see if Big Foot or something else went in or out.

They did not talk or move around much. P.J. read while Carlos watched carefully. From time to time P.J. took a turn with the field glasses.

Late in the afternoon P.J. smiled and said, "Carlos, we're not very smart. Big Foot won't come near where people live, at least not in the daytime."

Carlos said, "But we can't see anything go in or out of the cave at night from where we are now. We'll have to move closer."

P.J. said, "It will soon be dark. Then we'll move close to the rock where we can watch."

Carlos said sadly, "I hope Big Foot comes out before midnight. I hope it knows we have to go to work in the morning."

They laughed softly. P.J. said, "You sleep while I watch. Then we'll swap."

Shortly after dark they moved near to the cave. Carlos spread out his sleeping bag and lay on top of it. He was sound asleep when P.J. pushed him and said softly, "Carlos, wake up. I hear something coming this way."

Carlos woke up quickly. He asked, "Is it Big Foot?"

"I don't know. Let's be very quiet."

They could hear something moving along the ground closer and closer. Then it moved into the cave.

Carlos asked quietly, "When do we shine our lights on it?"

P.J. whispered, "After it comes out, and we follow it a little way."

"Let's get in a better spot to see the cave," Carlos said.

They moved carefully. Now they could see flashes of light in the cave. Then the light moved close to the entrance. They could see a large creature. They could hear it leaving the cave. They stepped behind the rock again. The creature walked across the rocky ground, making noise as it moved.

P.J. and Carlos followed until the creature reached the edge of the woods.

P.J. said softly, "Now, Carlos."

They were only a few feet from Big Foot.

This time he tore a mask from the face.

They flicked on their flashlights and ran toward it. Then it turned and began to run into the woods.

It was blinded by the lights and ran without looking. It hit a foot against a rock and fell forward. It lay on the ground without moving. Carlos and P.J. walked up and stood looking down at it. P.J. took his camera and snapped pictures.

The animal moved. Carlos suddenly reached down and grabbed the animal by the neck. He pulled hard. A large dark bunch of hair came off in his hands. He pulled again. This time he tore a mask from the face. Under the mask he found the face of their strange visitor.

"Mary Sue!" Carlos yelled.

"It's not a real Big Foot!" P.J. said.

The woman gave a loud growl. "You two bums again!" she yelled.

P.J. said to her. "We were just trying to find

a real Big Foot."

"We were looking for a big animal, not a person," Carlos said.

The woman was not so angry now. She stood up and said, "It's easy to fool some people. I fooled you two times."

"Why did you do this?" P.J. asked.

"Nothing interesting ever happens around here. Some woods have great trees like redwoods. Some have huge waterfalls. There was nothing around here like that. I decided to stir up some excitement. I didn't break the law," she said slowly.

"I know what you really wanted. You wanted us to report to a newspaper that we thought we had seen Big Foot," Carlos said in surprise.

"Yes, that's what I wanted. But you didn't report anything. All you did was come back and try to find it again," she said.

P.J. said, "Carlos, let's go home. I don't

want to be famous for finding a fake Big Foot."

Carlos said, "That's it. I'll never look for Big Foot again."

They walked away slowly. Mary Sue picked up her mask and headed home.

Carlos and P.J. came back to fish in Little River many times. They never told anyone about their adventure with Big Foot. But they laughed about it themselves many, many times.